MOONJINMEDIA

Reprinted and Distributed by Creative Teaching Press 2013
First Published December, 2010
Published by Moonjinmedia Co., Ltd.
www.moonjin.com

Text © 2010 Moonjinmedia Co., Ltd.
Illustrations © 2010 Donghoon Kim

ISBN 978-89-539-3426-9

e-CIP Homepage
http://www.nl.go.kr/cip.php
CIP: CIP2010003697

Itsy Bitsy Spider

Rozanne Lanczak Williams

Donghoon Kim

The itsy bitsy spider
Climbed up the water spout.
Down came the rain
And washed the spider out.

Out came the sun
And dried up all the rain.
And the itsy bitsy spider
Climbed up the spout again.

The itsy bitsy spider
Went down the garden path.
Here comes the water.
Oh, no! Splash! Splash!

The itsy bitsy spider
Climbed on a flower pot.
Safe from the water,
She found a nice, dry spot.

The itsy bitsy spider
Climbed up the shower wall.
Down came the water,
Just like a waterfall.

The itsy bitsy spider
Jumped out the shower door.
Then the itsy bitsy spider
Ran along the floor.

The itsy bitsy spider
Climbed on the kitchen sink.
Drip! Went the water
And the spider took a drink.

It was time to wash the dishes,
So the spider ran away.
She climbed into a tea cup,
And slept all day.

The itsy bitsy spider song
Is coming to an end.
The itsy bitsy spider
Finds an itsy bitsy friend.

Now two itsy bitsy spiders
Climb up to a tree.
They make their webs,
And sing their songs,
And live so happily!